Quentin Blake
SIMPKIN

PUFFIN

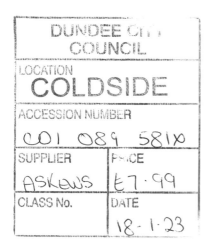
PUFFIN BOOKS

UK | USA | Canada | Ireland | Australia
India | New Zealand | South Africa

Puffin Books is part of the Penguin Random House group of companies whose addresses
can be found at global.penguinrandomhouse.com.

www.penguin.co.uk   www.puffin.co.uk   www.ladybird.co.uk

Penguin
Random House
UK

Jonathan Cape edition published 1993
Red Fox edition published 1995
Puffin Books edition published 2022
001

Printed in China

The authorized representative in the EEA is Penguin Random House Ireland, Morrison
Chambers, 32 Nassau Street, Dublin D02 YH68

A CIP catalogue record for this book is available from the British Library

ISBN: 978–0–241–62068–7

All correspondence to: Puffin Books, Penguin Random House Children's
One Embassy Gardens, 8 Viaduct Gardens, London SW11 7BW

MIX
Paper from
responsible sources
FSC® C018179

Here is
SIMPKIN

Simpkin
ONCE

and Simpkin
TWICE

Simpkin NASTY

Simpkin NICE

Simpkin FAST

and Simpkin SLOW

Simpkin HIGH

and Simpkin
LOW

Simpkin
ROUND and ROUND
the chairs

Simpkin UP

and DOWN the stairs

Simpkin THIN

and Simpkin FAT

Simpkin THIS

and Simpkin THAT

Simpkin WEAK

and Simpkin STRONG

Simpkin SHORT

and Simpkin LONG

Simpkin SMOOTH

and Simpkin ROUGH

and Simpkin

THAT IS QUITE ENOUGH

Simpkin WARM

and Simpkin CHILLY

Simpkin SENSIBLE

and
SILLY

And
sometimes
when
we
stand
and
call

Simpkin
JUST
NOT
THERE
AT
ALL